W9-ATT-379

This belongs to
_____
WITHDRAWN
Anne Arundel Co. Public Library

WITHDRAWN
Anne Arundel Co. Public Library

Copyright © 2021 by Milan Pavlović
Published in Canada and the USA in 2021 by Groundwood Books

All rights reserved. No part of this publication may be reproduced,
stored in a retrieval system or transmitted, in any form or by any
means, without the prior written consent of the publisher or a
license from The Canadian Copyright Licensing Agency (Access
Copyright). For an Access Copyright license, visit
www.accesscopyright.ca or call toll free to 1-800-893-5777.

Groundwood Books / House of Anansi Press
groundwoodbooks.com

Groundwood Books respectfully acknowledges that the land on
which we operate is the Traditional Territory of many Nations,
including the Anishinabeg, the Wendat and the Haudenosaunee. It
is also the Treaty Lands of the Mississaugas of the Credit.

We gratefully acknowledge for their financial support of our
publishing program the Canada Council for the Arts, the Ontario
Arts Council and the Government of Canada.

Library and Archives Canada Cataloguing in Publication
Title: Sonata for fish and boy / Milan Pavlović.
Names: Pavlović, Milan (Illustrator), author.
Identifiers: Canadiana (print) 20200296698 | Canadiana (ebook)
20200296728 | ISBN 9781773061610 (hardcover) | ISBN
9781773061627 (EPUB) | ISBN 9781773065168 (Kindle)
Classification: LCC PS8631.A8875 S66 2021 | DDC jC813/.6—dc23

The illustrations were created with colored inks and pencils on
watercolor paper.
Design by Michael Solomon
Printed and bound in Malaysia

Canada Council
for the Arts

Conseil des Arts
du Canada

ONTARIO ARTS COUNCIL
CONSEIL DES ARTS DE L'ONTARIO
an Ontario government agency
un organisme du gouvernement de l'Ontario

With the participation of the Government of Canada
Avec la participation du gouvernement du Canada | Canadä

MIX
Paper from
responsible sources
FSC® C012700

Sonata

For my wife, Jelena,
always and forever

for Fish and Boy

Milan Pavlović

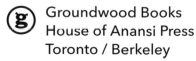
Groundwood Books
House of Anansi Press
Toronto / Berkeley